To the Hernandezes: Uncle George and Aunt Sherrill,
Uncle Joe and Aunt Mary Ann
—P. M. R.

For all my neighbors whose faces, houses, and
trees made their way into this book
—D. N.

Text copyright © 2005 by Pam Muñoz Ryan

Illustrations copyright © 2005 by Dennis Nolan

For information address Hyperion Books for Children, 114 Fifth Avenue, New York, New York 10011-5690.

Printed in Singapore

First Edition

1 3 5 7 9 10 8 6 4 2

This book is set in Centaur.

Reinforced binding

ISBN 0-7868-5492-8

Library of Congress Cataloging-in-Publication Data on file.

Visit www.hyperionbooksforchildren.com

There Was No Snow on Christmas Eve

By PAM MUÑOZ RYAN

Illustrations by DENNIS NOLAN

Hyperion Books for Children/*New York*

There was no snow on Christmas Eve
or snowflakes in a flurry dance.

No pristine banks of milky white
or ice pond in a shivery scene.

There was no bitter winter wind,
no need for woolen caps and gloves.

So long ago in Bethlehem,
instead of storm, a night serene.

There was no snow on Christmas Eve
when burro took them through the street.

Sweet Mary wore a flaxen robe
and Joseph, sandals on his feet.

A stable open to the world.
Their quilt? No more than supple straw.

The balmy season, bright with star,
let shepherds dream among the sheep.

There was no snow on Christmas Day.
Instead, a desert zephyr blew
and palm fronds sang a rustling tune,
to welcome the awaited birth.

Wise men and women, joy in heart,
Came humbly through the tranquil heat,

with barefoot children—all to see

why angels sang above the earth.